THE HOUSE OF LAVENDER

VALENTINA MARQUIS

DEDICATION

To all the drag queens across the globe—thank you. You teach us the art of resilience, the beauty of authenticity, and the courage of visibility. With every step on the stage, you challenge norms, inspire change, and celebrate the full spectrum of humanity with unparalleled brilliance and heart. This book is dedicated to you, the true heroes who transform not only themselves but the world around them, showing us all what it truly means to shine. Your light is a beacon for the brave and the bold. Thank you for leading the way with love, laughter, and fabulousness.

CONTENTS

PROLOGUE

In the heart of a bustling city, beneath the glow of a neon moon, the House of Lavender stood as a beacon of defiance and sanctuary. It was more than a home; it was a stage for the rejected, a shelter for the chased, and a gallery of the misunderstood. Here, among the fluttering curtains and the echoes of laughter, stories of courage and transformation were woven into the very walls, stitched between layers of silk and shadow.

Alex, a man who had once watched the world from the sidelines, found himself thrust into the spotlight under the most harrowing circumstances. Witnessing a crime that could cost him his life, he fled not into the darkness, but into the embrace of an unlikely refuge—a house filled with the boldest and brightest of drag queens. These queens did not just wear their scars as badges; they painted them in glitter and danced under spotlights, turning pain into a spectacle of strength.

But even as Alex began to stitch his life anew, the threads of his past tugged at him, dark figures lurking just beyond the stage lights, watching, waiting. The House of Lavender, with its vibrant occupants and its walls bursting with stories, taught him that to hide was not the same as to vanish. It taught him that the truest form of defiance was to be seen, fully and unapologetically.

This is a story of metamorphosis; of the masks we wear and the truths we unveil. It's about finding family in unexpected places and discovering that sometimes, the brightest light comes from the darkest of shadows. Welcome to the House of Lavender, where every echo has a story, and every shadow teaches us something about the light.

Chapter 1

A WITNESS IN DISGUISE

The Sapphire Lounge was a pulsing heart in the city's vibrant nightlife, throbbing with the latest beats and bathed in shimmering neon lights. Alex Masters leaned casually against the bar, his confident smile complemented by the tailored fit of his shirt that hinted at a well-maintained physique. He was in his element, surrounded by the weekend crowd of carefree dancers and hopeful romantics.

As he flirted effortlessly with a woman whose laughter mingled perfectly with the rhythm of the music, a sudden shift in the atmosphere caught his attention. The air grew tense, a stark contrast to the light-hearted revelry. Curiosity piqued, Alex excused himself with a charming wink and made his way through the dense crowd toward the commotion at the back of the club.

Hidden by the shadows, he watched in horror as a grim scene unfolded. A man, whose expensive suit did little to conceal his dangerous demeanor, pressed a gun against the forehead of a trembling club-goer. The gun's cold gleam was the only warning before it discharged, a sound muffled by the music yet unmistakably deadly. The body hit the ground with a thud that echoed in Alex's ears.

The killer's eyes, cold and calculating, swept the area and locked onto Alex. Heart pounding, Alex realized he had been seen witnessing the murder. He was now a target.

Before he could process his next move, the wail of police sirens filled the air, growing louder as they approached. Panic set in around him as clubbers screamed and scrambled, but Alex found himself gripped firmly by the arm. He turned to face a plain-clothes police officer, who quickly flashed a badge.

"Alex Masters? You're in danger. We need to move you now," the officer stated, urgency clear in his voice.

Pushed through the panicked crowd, Alex

was escorted out of the club and into the chilly night air. He barely had time to register the coolness against his skin before being bundled into an unmarked black SUV. The vehicle sped away, leaving behind the chaos and the flashing lights of police cars now swarming the club.

Inside the SUV, the atmosphere was tense. "The Mendoza Cartel doesn't take kindly to witnesses. You saw their hitman's face; you're a loose end they'll want to tie up fast," the female officer explained as she navigated through the city's streets.

"We're taking you somewhere no one would think to look for you," her partner added, giving Alex a sympathetic look. "The House of Lavender. It's a safe house of sorts, in its own unique way."

Alex, still processing the night's shocking events, frowned. "The House of Lavender? What is that, some kind of spa?"

"It's a house full of drag queens," the woman replied without missing a beat, checking her mirrors for tails. "They're gearing up for a major competition. You'll blend in better than you think."

As the SUV pulled up to a brightly painted Victorian mansion adorned with glittering lights and flamboyant decorations, Alex's apprehension grew. The sound of music and laughter spilled out as the door opened, clashing with the grim reality of his situation.

Standing at the entrance was Miss Electra, a vision in sequins and perfectly coiffed hair, who regarded Alex with a mix of amusement and scrutiny. "Welcome to the House of Lavender, darling. I'm Miss Electra, and I'll be your guardian angel—or devil, depending on how cooperative you are."

Alex hesitated, discomfort mounting. "Look, I appreciate the help, but I'm not going to—"

"Honey, by the time we're done, even the mirror won't recognize you," Miss Electra interjected with a wink, guiding him inside. "For now, let's focus on keeping you alive. We can argue about wardrobe choices later."

As the evening unfolded, Alex found himself drawn into an unexpected world.

The queens were not only artists but warriors in their own right, each with a story more compelling than the last. Surrounded by their strength and solidarity, Alex's initial biases began to crumble, revealing the first cracks in his armor.

Chapter 2

NEW REFUGE

Alex stepped over the threshold of the House of Lavender, his senses immediately assaulted by a cacophony of sights, sounds, and smells. Glitter seemed to be a structural element here, and the air was a heady mix of perfume, hairspray, and something that suspiciously smelled like burnt toast.

Miss Electra, seeing his wide-eyed bewilderment, looped her arm through his. "Welcome to the madhouse, darling. First rule of drag—never let them see you sweat… unless it's under stage lights."

As they walked through the hallway,

portraits of drag legends stared down at him, their eyes following every bewildered tourist like a lineup of judgy aunts at a family reunion. The walls were a vibrant patchwork of feather boas and sequined dresses.

In the main living room, a group of drag queens were huddled around a laptop, watching a performance video. They looked up as Miss Electra announced, "Ladies and gentlemen and those who refuse to conform, meet our new houseguest—Alex, the accidental voyeur."

A queen with eyelashes so long they could've been used as feather dusters batted her eyes at Alex. "Ooh, a spy. How very James Bond. Except our Bond here got caught on his first mission."

"Honey, around here, we don't get caught; we get applause," quipped another, her makeup so bright and colorful it could have directed airport traffic.

Alex, unsure how to respond, managed a tight smile. Miss Electra pushed him gently forward. "Don't worry, they're just teasing. We're all family here—dysfunctional, sure, but family nonetheless."

She led him to what would be his room. It was less a room and more an explosion in a paint factory. "You'll be staying with Tanya Tuck. She's out buying… more glitter, I presume. But make yourself at home!"

As he sat on the bed, a spring squeaked

ominously. "Great," Alex muttered, "even the furniture has a sense of humor here."

Later, during dinner—a concoction that defied culinary categorization—Alex tried to blend in. The queens shared stories of their first times on stage, each tale more hilarious and heartwarming than the last.

When it was his turn to share something, Alex decided to try humor. "Well, the first time I dressed up was for a Halloween party. I went as a 'broke college student'— wore my regular clothes and carried a textbook. I won 'Most Realistic Costume.'"

The table erupted in laughter. Miss Electra nodded approvingly. "See, you're getting the hang of it. Around here, if you can laugh at yourself, you're golden."

As the night wore on, Alex began to feel less like an outsider. The laughter, the stories, and even the bizarre dinner started to make this strange new world feel a little bit like home.

Chapter 3

DRAG 101 TO A CLOSE CALL

Alex woke up to the sound of Beyoncé's "Run the World" blasting through the House of Lavender. Groaning, he buried his face into the pillow. Apparently, here, 'quiet mornings' were a myth right up there with 'low-calorie cheesecake.' As he stumbled into the hallway, Alex was swept into an impromptu dance routine led by Miss Electra, who seemed to believe morning exercise should feel like a Broadway audition.

"Think of it as coffee for the soul," Electra

said, thrusting a feather boa into his hands and pulling him into the fray. Alex's two left feet made him a standout, but not in a way one might hope.

The queens were preparing for a big event—the regional drag competition known as "The Glitter Gala." Alex was assigned to embody David Bowie, mixing glam rock with high heels. He practiced his strut, which more closely resembled a stagger, much to the amusement of his housemates. "Darling, the secret is to glide, not collide," Tanya Tuck advised, demonstrating a walk that somehow perfectly balanced dignity and a physics-defying wig.

One afternoon, Alex's education continued with a crash course in lip-syncing. "The key is to mime with passion," instructed Glitter Gary. "Pretend you're convincing a deaf grandmother you're not hungry." Alex's attempts started rocky but eventually, his mouthing could have fooled even the most critical lip-reader at a silent opera.

Next came the high heels challenge. Alex was handed stilettos so tall they should have come with a warning label and oxygen. His initial attempt at walking was less catwalk, more toddler-on-ice. The queens gathered, offering 'supportive' commentary. "Honey, it looks like you're trying to stomp out invisible ants," joked Divina DeCampo.

 the days rolled on, Alex grew more adept, and his relationships within the house deepened. These bonds were tested one evening when Tanya, peering out a window, spotted a suspicious figure lurking near the garden. The house's response was swift—lights out, everyone in one room, breaths held. The figure turned out to be just a nosy neighbor curious about the commotion typically surrounding their infamous home, but the scare left a mark, prompting the installation of security cameras.

With "The Glitter Gala" looming, the incident momentarily united them in a bout of protective paranoia that somehow morphed into a spirited debate about the best diva defenses—ranging from Whitney Houston's high notes as an auditory shield to Madonna's pointed bra as literal armor.

On the night of the gala, Alex, decked out in a Ziggy Stardust ensemble complete with glitter and gusto, took to the stage. If nerves were butterflies, he was a walking sanctuary. Yet, as the music started, something magical happened. Alex transformed. His movements, once awkward, now carried the confidence and flair of a seasoned queen. His performance was not just an imitation but a tribute, earning roars of approval from an audience that included his new family, cheering the loudest.

Post-competition, the queens returned to their sanctuary, trophies in hand and hearts full. They celebrated not just their third-place victory but the journey they'd shared. Alex, once an outsider, now found himself amid genuine laughter, quirky family banter, and a sense of belonging that was as surprising as it was delightful.

Chapter 4

UNDER THE GLITTER

The House of Lavender was buzzing with excitement and nerves as the queens prepared for the regional drag competition, known among the community as "The Glitter Gala." This annual event was a spectacle of sequins, songs, and sass, and for the first time, Alex was not just a bystander but a participant. Miss Electra, ever the maternal figure in stilettos, had decided Alex was ready for more than just watching from the sidelines.

Alex was assigned a segment that would pay tribute to the legendary David Bowie. His task was not just to impersonate but to channel the icon, blending Bowie's androgynous glam rock with the exaggerated femininity of drag. The preparation involved was intense; it included everything from mastering Bowie's distinct vocal stylings to adopting his ethereal, otherworldly poise. Alex practiced walking in his glittery platform boots around the house, trying to keep his balance while Tanya Tuck offered tips on how to turn a stumble into part of the performance—"Make it part of the dance, darling, every falter is a step in disguise!"

As the competition day drew near, the house's usual banter was mixed with bouts of frenzied costume fittings and last-minute changes to routines. One evening, as they were all gathered around the cluttered dining table covered in fabric and feathers, the atmosphere was electric with creativity and camaraderie.

Miss Electra, overseeing the chaos like a general in the field, couldn't help but notice Alex's growing confidence. "Look at you, my boy, almost ready to snatch the crown yourself," she teased as she adjusted a sparkling choker around his neck.

However, not all was glitter and glam. The night before the gala, as Alex was perfecting his makeup in the mirror, he caught a shadow moving outside the window. His heart skipped a beat. Peering into the darkness, he saw nothing but felt uneasy. He decided to mention it to Miss Electra, who heightened security, adding a note of tension to the air.

The day of "The Glitter Gala" finally arrived, and the queens loaded into their van, a vehicle as flamboyant as its passengers, decked out in pink and purple, with lashes drawn over the headlights. Alex felt a mixture of excitement and nerves churn in his stomach as they approached the venue, a grand old theater that smelled of history and hairspray.

Backstage, the queens helped each other with last touches of makeup and costume adjustments. Alex, now fully transformed into his Bowie persona, felt a strange calmness settle over him. He looked around at his new family, their faces illuminated by the soft glow of vanity mirrors, and felt an overwhelming sense of pride and belonging.

When it was his turn to perform, Alex stepped onto the stage with a presence he had never known he possessed. The spotlight hit him, and for a moment, he was no longer Alex but Stardust incarnates. His performance was a mesmerizing blend of music and movement, capturing the essence of Bowie so vividly that the audience was left in awe.

The applause was thunderous, the cheers filled with genuine admiration. As he walked off the stage, his heart was pounding not just from the performance but from the realization of how much he had changed since arriving at the House of Lavender. He was no longer the man who had stumbled into the house; he was part of something bigger, something beautiful.

As the queens celebrated their performance, regardless of the outcome, they gathered around Alex, lifting him onto their shoulders. "To Alex, the star who fell to earth and rose as one of us!" Miss Electra exclaimed, and the room erupted in cheers.

Back at the house, the mood was jubilant. They had placed third, a respectable position given the fierce competition. But more importantly, they had triumphed in their own right, with Alex now truly one of them, shining under the glitter.

Chapter 5

ECHOES OF DANGER

Fresh off their triumphant return from "The Glitter Gala," the mood at the House of Lavender was one of jubilant celebration mixed with relief. The queens had not only proven themselves on the stage but had also deepened their bonds as a chosen family. Amidst the laughter and storytelling that followed, Alex felt an overwhelming sense of belonging. He had transformed from an outsider seeking refuge to an integral member of this vibrant community.

In the days that followed, life at the House of Lavender resumed its usual rhythm of rehearsals and revelry. Alex, now more comfortable in his heels than ever, joined Miss Electra for morning coffee, a new ritual that included reviewing performance tapes and discussing the nuances of stage presence. It was during one of these sessions that Miss Electra turned the conversation towards a more serious topic.

"You know, darling, the stage isn't just about the spotlight. It's also about the shadows it casts," she mused, her eyes reflecting a mix of wisdom and warning. "Always be aware of what's lurking in them." Her words, though cryptic, reminded Alex of the ever-present danger that hovered just outside their colorful sanctuary.

The reminder of his precarious situation

became starkly real one afternoon when Alex noticed a series of missed calls on his burner phone—the one given to him by the police for emergencies. The calls were from an unknown number, and a knot of anxiety tightened in his stomach. He decided to ignore them, but the seed of unease had been planted.

That evening, as the house prepared for an impromptu drag show in their backyard— a glittering affair meant to thank their local supporters—Alex couldn't shake the feeling of being watched. The towering fences and newly installed security cameras offered little reassurance. His concerns were shared in hushed tones with Tanya Tuck, who had become his confidante.

"We've got eyes everywhere, and yet, it feels like we're the ones being seen," Alex whispered as they adjusted their costumes. Tanya, ever the pragmatist, patted his shoulder with a reassuring smile.

"Then let's give them a show they won't forget," she quipped, her optimism a stark contrast to Alex's growing worry.

As night fell and the backyard filled with an enthusiastic crowd, the show kicked off with the usual flair. Alex, dressed in his most dazzling outfit yet, performed with a vigor that belied his internal turmoil. The crowd's cheers washed over him, a temporary balm to his fears.

However, midway through the show, Alex spotted a figure at the back of the crowd, partially hidden by shadows. The figure was pointing what looked like a camera in his direction. Heart pounding, Alex signaled to Miss Electra, who subtly maneuvered the performance to block the view.

The figure soon disappeared, but the incident left a chilling impact, cutting the evening's festivities short. The queens gathered inside; their laughter replaced by concerned murmurs.

"We need to tighten security. This isn't just about winning crowns anymore," Miss Electra declared, her usual flamboyance tempered by the weight of her responsibility.

The next day, the local police were called

in to review the footage from the security cameras. Although they could not conclusively identify the mysterious figure, they agreed to increase patrols around the area.

Reassured but not relaxed, Alex spent the following days reflecting on his journey. He had embraced a new identity, found courage in heels, and discovered a family in the most unexpected of places. Yet, the shadow of danger reminded him that his transformation was not without its risks.

As Alex looked around at the colorful walls of the House of Lavender, each adorned with portraits of drag legends past and present, he realized that their legacy was not just about the glitz and glamor but also about resilience in the face of adversity. He was determined to uphold that legacy, come what may.

Chapter 6

SPOTLIGHT AND SHADOWS

The House of Lavender had never been just a home; it was a fortress of feathers and sequins, where every laugh was a defiance of the darker world outside. As the weeks passed, the shadow that lingered over Alex grew, but so did his resolve and attachment to his newfound family. Miss Electra, sensing his anxiety mixed with determination, took it upon herself to mentor him not just in the arts of drag, but in the arts of resilience.

One brisk morning, while the house still slumbered, Alex found himself sipping coffee with Miss Electra in the kitchen, a rare quiet moment in the otherwise bustling house. "You know, darling, the brighter the spotlight, the darker the shadows," Miss Electra said, her voice soft but serious. "But remember, shadows only mean there's a light shining somewhere. Don't let the dark parts scare you too much."

Their conversation was interrupted by a raucous laughter coming from the living room where Tanya Tuck and Glitter Gary were attempting to choreograph a new number, involving a disco ball, two feather boas, and a unicycle. The absurdity of the scene brought a smile to Alex's face, a reminder of why this place had become so dear to him.

Later that day, the house received an

invitation to perform at a high-profile charity ball, an event that promised not only to raise funds for local LGBTQ+ charities but also to elevate the House of Lavender's status in the drag community. The queens buzzed with excitement, throwing themselves into preparations. Alex was tasked with a solo performance, a tribute to musical legends, which would be his most public appearance yet.

As the event approached, rehearsals intensified. Alex spent hours in the studio, his body moving to the rhythm of the music, his mind occasionally drifting to the mysterious figure who had been watching him. The fear of being discovered by the cartel loomed over him, but the applause and laughter from his sisters during rehearsals reminded him of what he was fighting for—freedom, in more ways than one.

The night of the charity ball arrived, and the House of Lavender queens made their entrance, draped in their most extravagant outfits. The venue was a grand ballroom, adorned with chandeliers and elegant drapery, filled with the city's elite. Alex, dressed as Freddie Mercury, felt the adrenaline surge as he stepped onto the stage. His performance was a dazzling display of vocal prowess and theatrical flair, earning him a standing ovation.

However, amid the applause, Alex's eyes caught a figure retreating through a side door—a man whose gaze had lingered a little too long. His heart skipped a beat. Was the cartel here? He excused himself from the celebrations and followed discreetly, only to find the man handing out flyers for another event. Relief washed over Alex, though it was tinged with frustration at his own paranoia.

Back at the party, the queens celebrated their success, unaware of Alex's brief scare. They returned home in the early hours, spirits high, laughter filling the van. Yet, as the city lights blurred past, Alex's thoughts were somber. The evening had been a triumph, but each public appearance was a risk. He realized that while he could embrace his new persona on stage, he had to guard his true identity more carefully than ever.

In the coming days, Alex took steps to enhance his security, changing his routines and keeping a lower profile when outside the House of Lavender. He knew he couldn't let his guard down, not when so much was at stake. Yet, amidst the fear and caution, Alex found strength in the spotlight, the cheers of the crowd a reminder that he was not just hiding; he was thriving, shadows and all.

Chapter 7

REFLECTIONS AND REVELATIONS

As autumn descended on the city, the House of Lavender became a hive of activity, preparing for the upcoming drag festival—a highlight of their calendar and an event that promised to bring together the brightest stars of the drag community. Amid the whirlwind of preparations, Alex found himself more introspective, the recent events having stirred a deeper contemplation about his journey and the path that lay ahead.

One chilly evening, while sorting through an array of costumes in the attic with Miss

Electra, Alex stumbled upon an old photo album filled with pictures of drag queens from decades past. The two settled into a sea of velvet and lace, flipping through the pages. Miss Electra narrated tales of each queen, her voice tinged with nostalgia and pride. "These were the pioneers, darling," she said, pointing to a black-and-white photo of a queen who radiated confidence and defiance. "They paved the runway we strut on today."

Inspired by the stories, Alex felt a renewed sense of purpose. The dangers he faced seemed less formidable when cast in the light of these trailblazers' struggles and triumphs. It was during these moments of vulnerability and shared history that Alex truly appreciated the depth of the legacy he was becoming a part of.

The preparation for the festival continued, with each queen contributing their unique flair and expertise. Alex, who had grown in both skill and confidence, was given the honor of designing a segment of the show. He chose to create a performance that would celebrate the history of drag, weaving in elements from the stories Miss Electra had shared. It was a project that felt deeply personal, and he poured his heart into choreographing each step and selecting each song.

As the festival approached, a nervous excitement permeated the House of Lavender. The night before the event, the queens gathered in the living room, their faces illuminated by the soft glow of the fireplace. They shared their hopes and dreams for the festival, each voice adding to a tapestry of collective ambition and individual aspiration. Alex listened, his heart swelling with affection and admiration for these extraordinary individuals who had become his family.

The day of the festival dawned clear and bright, the crisp air filled with the scent of autumn leaves. The venue was a kaleidoscope of color and sound, with queens from across the region descending in a dazzling array of costumes. Alex's segment was a hit, the audience moved by the homage to the drag queens of yesteryear. His performance, a blend of vintage glamour and modern edge, received thunderous applause, affirming his place in this vibrant community.

However, amid the celebrations, Alex's

eyes were constantly scanning the crowd, the fear of being recognized by someone from his past never far from his mind. His paranoia was heightened when he noticed a few unfamiliar faces lingering near the stage, their expressions unreadable. His concern grew when one of them was seen talking to a security guard, gesturing subtly towards where Alex was signing autographs.

The incident cast a shadow over the evening, and despite the success of the festival, Alex returned home with a heavy heart. He confided his fears to Miss Electra, who listened intently before offering her usual blend of comfort and pragmatic advice. "We can't let fear dictate our lives, but we must be smart, savvy, and prepared," she said, her hand resting reassuringly on his shoulder.

That night, Alex lay awake, reflecting on the day's events and the precarious balance of his life—celebrated on stage yet concealed in the shadows. It was a dichotomy that he was still learning to navigate, each day presenting new challenges and reaffirming his resolve to not only survive but thrive.

Chapter 8

THE UNSEEN THREADS

The weeks following the drag festival were a whirlwind of accolades and anxiety for Alex. The festival had not only been a triumph for the House of Lavender but had also catapulted Alex into the spotlight, earning him invitations to guest perform at various high-profile venues across the city. While this recognition thrilled him, it also amplified his fears of exposure. Each cheer from the audience was mirrored by a whisper of caution in the back of his mind.

As autumn deepened, the days grew shorter

and the nights longer, lending an eerie quiet to the evenings at the House of Lavender. It was during one such night, while practicing his routine in the dimly lit studio, that Alex noticed a flicker of movement outside the window. Peering into the darkness, he saw nothing but the rustling of the autumn leaves. The moment, though fleeting, left him rattled, a stark reminder of the danger that lurked just beyond the stage lights.

Determined to not let fear overshadow his achievements, Alex threw himself into his work with renewed vigor. He designed a new act that would not only dazzle with its creativity but also serve as a cathartic release from the mounting pressure. The act, a dramatic interpretation of a phoenix rising from the ashes, was both a metaphor for his own resurgence and a defiant response to the threats he faced.

Meanwhile, the camaraderie within the House of Lavender grew stronger. Miss Electra, always perceptive, took note of Alex's heightened anxiety and organized a weekend retreat for the house. The getaway, set in a secluded cabin surrounded by the serene beauty of nature, was a chance for everyone to unwind and bond away from the chaos of the city.

During the retreat, around a crackling campfire under the starlit sky, the queens shared stories of their own fears and how they overcame them. Alex listened, his heart heavy but hopeful, drawing strength from the collective resilience of his newfound family. It was during this intimate gathering that he realized no matter how challenging the path, he was not walking it alone.

One evening, after returning from the retreat, Alex received an anonymous note slipped under his door. The message was cryptic, a simple quote: "The brightest flames cast the darkest shadows." The note, unsigned and unsettling, spurred a mixture of motivation and dread within him. Was it a warning, a threat, or perhaps an encouragement from a secret admirer aware of his struggles?

The following days were tinged with a sense of cautious watchfulness. Alex and the queens reviewed their security measures, ensuring that their sanctuary remained protected. Despite the undercurrent of tension, life at the House of Lavender continued with its usual flair for the dramatic and fabulous.

On a brisk evening, as Alex prepared for a major performance at a city gala, he reflected on the note's message. Dressed in his phoenix costume, feathers adorned with shimmering stones, he stood backstage, the weight of the moment settling on his shoulders. As he stepped into the spotlight, the cheers of the crowd swelling around him, Alex felt a surge of empowerment. With each move, each note, he shed the weight of his fears, his performance a blazing testament to his journey from the ashes of his past to the brilliance of his present.

Backstage, after the curtains fell and the

applause died down, Alex felt a profound shift within him. The threats, while not diminished, seemed less daunting. He knew the road ahead would be fraught with challenges, but he was ready to face them with the courage and support of his drag family.

Chapter 9

A DANCE WITH SHADOWS

After his phoenix performance, which had ignited the hearts of many and further established his burgeoning reputation, Alex found himself at a crossroads of celebration and caution. The gala performance had been a triumph, and offers for appearances and interviews began pouring in, each promising greater exposure—a double-edged sword that Alex was increasingly wary of wielding.

As autumn gave way to the biting chill of early winter, the House of Lavender was abuzz with preparations for the upcoming holiday season, a time traditionally marked by extravagant shows and festive extravagance. The queens decorated the house with an array of twinkling lights, colorful garlands, and a towering Christmas tree that sparkled from every angle. Despite the festive atmosphere, Alex couldn't shake the lingering anxiety that had taken root in his mind since the anonymous note and his recent brush with danger.

During a particularly frosty evening, while Alex was rehearsing in the main hall, adorned with holiday decor that made every corner glisten, he received a call from an unknown number. Hesitating only for a moment, he answered, his voice steady. The caller was a journalist from a well-known entertainment magazine, eager to feature Alex in an upcoming issue. The opportunity was tempting, a chance to tell his story on his own terms, yet every instinct screamed that it could also lead to exposure he couldn't afford.

Later that night, while the queens celebrated the successful planning of their New Year's Eve show, Alex retreated to the quiet of his room, the weight of his decision pressing down on him. He turned the journalist's offer over in his mind, considering all the angles, but found no clear path forward. His desire to embrace his newfound identity clashed painfully with his need to remain hidden.

Seeking guidance, Alex confided in Miss Electra, who listened with a grave seriousness that was rare for her usually vibrant demeanor. "Darling, the spotlight is a fickle friend. It can warm you with its glow but burn you just as quickly," she said, her eyes reflecting the flicker of the fireplace. "You must decide if the warmth is worth the burn."

The next day brought no relief. While out for a brief walk to clear his head, Alex noticed a suspicious car parked across from the House of Lavender. The same car had been there the previous two days, its occupants obscured but intent. A cold dread settled in his stomach as he hurried back inside, the festive lights of the house now seeming more like a beacon than a decoration.

That evening, with the house quiet except for the soft sounds of holiday music playing in the background, Alex sat down with the rest of the queens. He laid out his fears, the recent odd occurrences, and the looming decision about the interview. The group listened intently, their usual joviality replaced by a shared concern. They discussed various strategies, from increasing security to possibly declining the interview, each option weighed with the seriousness it deserved.

As they talked, Alex felt the strength of his bond with the queens, their support a tangible force that bolstered his resolve. They decided, together, that Alex would proceed with the interview, but with careful measures in place to protect his identity and location. The decision was made not just for the sake of his career but as a stand against the fear that sought to control him.

Emboldened by the collective decision, Alex spent the following weeks preparing for the interview and the New Year's Eve show, his days a blend of excitement and meticulous planning. The interview would be his chance to showcase not just his talent but his courage, the story he chose to tell one of resilience and defiance, a narrative thread spun from the very fabric of the House of Lavender itself.

Chapter 10

THE ECHOES OF COURAGE

As winter's grip tightened around the city, Alex found himself at the epicenter of a whirlwind of activity. The interview had been set, and the reporter had promised discretion, but the ripple effects of his growing fame were impossible to ignore. With each passing day, as the New Year's Eve show approached, Alex felt the dual edges of excitement and trepidation sharpening.

The House of Lavender was alive with the spirit of the season, draped in garlands and shimmering with lights. The queens, ever supportive, rallied around Alex, their own preparations for the holiday festivities intertwining with efforts to ensure his upcoming interview would cast him in the light he deserved, without exposing him to the dangers he feared.

Amid this bustling backdrop, Alex spent long nights perfecting his performance for New Year's Eve, a piece he hoped would encapsulate his journey of transformation and defiance. The routine was a bold mix of dance and dramatic monologue, a narrative arc that mirrored his own life's recent chapters. Every leap and line delivered on stage was a cathartic release of his pent-up fears and a celebration of his newfound identity.

However, as the final rehearsals drew to a

close, an unsettling incident threatened to unravel the threads of security they had so carefully woven. During a late-night costume fitting session, a brick wrapped in a note crashed through one of the front windows of the House of Lavender. The note was stark and threatening: "Stay out of the spotlight or suffer the consequences." The house fell into a tense silence, the broken glass a chilling reminder of the vulnerability that fame could bring.

Shaken but not deterred, the queens gathered in the living room, the site of many previous celebrations now turned into a crisis meeting point. Miss Electra, her usual flamboyance tempered by the gravity of the situation, laid out their options with a calm resolve. "We can either let this threat push us back into the shadows, or we can stand up and shine brighter," she declared, her voice firm and inspiring.

The decision was unanimous. They would not be intimidated into silence. Instead, they would use the New Year's Eve show as a platform to demonstrate their unity and resilience. Security measures were doubled, and local authorities were alerted to the threat, ensuring that their celebration would be safeguarded.

The night of the show arrived, crisp and clear, with a blanket of snow adding a pristine beauty to the landscape. The venue was packed, a sea of faces illuminated by anticipation and the soft glow of candlelight tables. As Alex stepped onto the stage, his heart was pounding, not just from nerves but from the weight of the moment.

His performance began in darkness, a single spotlight slowly rising to reveal him standing alone. The music swelled, a haunting melody that filled the room, and Alex moved, each step and word painting a picture of struggle and triumph. The audience was captivated, drawn into his world, feeling every emotion conveyed through his artful expression.

As the final notes of his performance echoed through the hall, the audience erupted into applause, a standing ovation that reverberated like a heartbeat through the venue. Alex bowed, tears glistening in his eyes, overwhelmed by the support and love that filled the room.

Backstage, the queens embraced him, their congratulations mingled with relief. The night had been a resounding success, and more importantly, it had passed without incident. The threat had been faced, and though it had not been vanquished, it had been defied.

As the new year rang in, with cheers and the clinking of glasses, Alex looked around at the faces of his family—the House of Lavender—and felt a profound sense of gratitude. They had turned what could have been a night of fear into a celebration of life and art. And while the future was uncertain, one thing was clear: whatever shadows might loom, they would face them together, as a family united not just by circumstance, but by choice and by the unbreakable bonds of love and courage.

Chapter 11

TURNING TIDES

In the aftermath of the New Year's Eve show, the members of the House of Lavender felt a renewed sense of solidarity and purpose. The successful night had not only been a testament to their collective resilience but also a defiant stand against the threats that sought to undermine their spirits. The warmth of their triumph lingered as the cold winter continued to embrace the city outside.

Despite the external bravado, the incident with the brick had left a subtle but undeniable mark on Alex. He found himself looking over his shoulder more often, and the ring of the phone filled him with a momentary dread before he could remind himself that he was surrounded by allies and protectors. His interview with the journalist was due to be published soon, and while he had managed to navigate the questions with care, ensuring that nothing too revealing about his location or past was disclosed, the anticipation of its release brought a mixture of excitement and anxiety.

The House of Lavender did not slow down; if anything, it buzzed with even more activity. Miss Electra, ever the matriarch, organized a series of workshops and events not only to keep everyone's spirits up but also to foster a deeper connection with the local community. These events ranged from makeup tutorials open to the public, charity fundraisers, to intimate performances that showcased the diverse talents within the house. Alex threw himself into these activities, finding that each event helped to distract him from his worries and deepen his bonds with the others.

During one such workshop, Alex met a young fan, a timid teenager who reminded him starkly of himself at that age. The boy, named Jamie, shared his own struggles with acceptance and identity, and Alex found himself moved by the courage it took the young fan to reach out. They spoke at length, and Alex offered words of encouragement, feeling a surge of protectiveness and kinship that he hadn't anticipated.

As the day of the interview's publication drew nearer, tension within the house grew palpable. The queens, while supportive, also prepared for any potential backlash. Security protocols were reviewed and reinforced, and everyone was on high alert. When the article finally went live, it was met with a wave of support that far exceeded their worries. Readers from around the country sent messages of solidarity and admiration for Alex's bravery and openness.

Emboldened by the positive reception, Alex began to feel more confident about his place in the public eye. He realized that each expression of support was a shield against the threats he faced, a collective affirmation that he was not alone.

However, amidst the celebration, a less welcome message arrived. An anonymous email made its way to Alex's inbox late one evening, its contents a stark reminder of the danger still lurking in the shadows. "You can shine as brightly as you want, but shadows are always waiting," it read. The message sent a chill down Alex's spine, and he immediately informed Miss Electra.

Gathering in the privacy of her office, Alex, Miss Electra, and a few of the senior queens discussed their next steps. They decided to involve the police, who took the threat seriously and began an investigation. The house's security system was upgraded, and personal safety measures for each member, especially Alex, were tightened.

Despite these precautions, Alex felt a

change within himself. The constant threats had begun to forge a new layer of resilience in him. He was more determined than ever to not let fear dictate his life. Inspired by the support he received, he started working on a new performance piece, one that symbolized the journey from fear to fortitude, a narrative he hoped would inspire others just as he had been inspired by his community and fans.

As winter slowly melted into the first hints of spring, Alex watched the ice thawing in the garden of the House of Lavender, seeing in it a metaphor for his own thawing fears. He knew challenges lay ahead, but he also knew he had a family, a purpose, and a voice that would not be silenced.

Chapter 12

LEGACY OF LIGHT

As spring ushered in renewal and growth, so too did it bring a season of reflection and bold decisions for Alex. The house of Lavender, vibrant with the fresh blooms of tulips and daffodils that adorned its gardens, mirrored the rejuvenation felt by its inhabitants. Alex, in particular, found himself at a pivotal juncture. The threats, though still a dark cloud on the horizon, had somewhat receded in the face of his and the house's increased security measures and the police's ongoing investigations.

The warm reception of his interview had

not only bolstered his confidence but had also opened new avenues for him. Invitations for more public appearances, interviews, and even talks about a potential book deal were now part of his daily correspondences. Each opportunity was a step further into the spotlight, a place he had once feared but was now learning to navigate with the grace of a seasoned performer.

Amidst this whirlwind of opportunities, Alex dedicated time to crafting his new performance piece, which he titled "Echoes of Light." It was a deeply personal narrative, exploring the themes of fear, resilience, and the transformative power of acceptance. The piece was set to debut at the city's annual Pride festival, a perfect venue for such a powerful message.

Meanwhile, the House of Lavender thrived with activity as the queens prepared for the festival. Costumes, choreography, and set designs filled every corner of the house with a chaotic but creative energy. Miss Electra, seeing the potential in Alex's new project, gave him full creative control over a segment of their festival performance. This trust and responsibility were both an honor and a challenge that Alex accepted with eager determination.

During rehearsals, Alex's piece came to life. It featured a blend of dramatic monologues, interpretive dance, and powerful music that moved all who watched, even in its raw form. The other queens contributed their talents, helping to refine the choreography and enhance the visual elements of the performance. It was collaborative creativity at its finest, and Alex felt a profound gratitude for the family he had found in the House of Lavender.

One afternoon, as he walked through the bustling streets to meet with a local author about his potential book, Alex felt a sense of accomplishment that had once seemed impossible. He had not only faced his fears but was using them to fuel his journey forward. However, as he sat in the café, discussing chapters and narratives, his phone buzzed with a reminder of the fragile balance he still maintained. It was a text from Miss Electra, brief but urgent: "Come home. Need to talk."

Rushing back, Alex found the house unusually quiet. In the living room, the queens gathered, their expressions somber. Miss Electra handed him a letter that had been delivered that morning. It was more direct than the previous threats, a detailed warning that discussed Alex's recent public appearances and hinted at consequences if he continued to step into the public eye.

The room filled with tension as they discussed their options. The threat was no longer just an anonymous shadow; it was becoming a direct challenge to Alex's newfound life and visibility. The discussion was intense, with some queens advocating for more privacy and others, including Alex, insisting that retreating from public view would mean giving in to fear.

After much debate, they reached a

consensus. They would not cancel the Pride performance or any other public engagements. Instead, they would increase their security measures even further and coordinate closely with local law enforcement. They agreed that the visibility Alex had gained should be used as a platform not just for his art but also for advocacy against the kind of hatred and intolerance that the threats represented.

As spring turned to summer, the Pride festival approached, and Alex's segment, "Echoes of Light," was ready. It was more than just a performance; it was a declaration, a beacon for anyone who had ever felt overshadowed by fear. Standing backstage, ready to step into the flood of stage lights, Alex felt the full weight of the moment. This was not just his story; it was a story shared by many, and he was ready to tell it, come what may.

Chapter 13

VOICES OF VALOR

As the city buzzed with the vibrant colors and sounds of the upcoming Pride festival, Alex's heart was a mix of anticipation and nerves. "Echoes of Light" was more than a performance; it was his manifesto, his rebellion against the shadows that had chased him since that fateful night he witnessed a crime that changed his life forever. Now, as he stood on the brink of revealing his soul to the world, he felt every eye, every expectation, weighing on him like never before.

The Pride festival was a kaleidoscope of joy, a celebration of diversity and unity that stretched across the city's heart. The streets were lined with flags, the air filled with music, and the people—a vibrant sea of individuals sharing a common cause of love and acceptance. The House of Lavender, decked out in all its flamboyant glory, became a beacon for many, with Alex as one of its shining lights.

Despite the jubilant atmosphere, the weight of the recent threats lingered in Alex's mind. Security was tighter than ever; plainclothes officers mingled with the crowd, and every entrance and exit was monitored. The queens, too, were vigilant, their usual carefree spirits tempered by a protective streak, especially towards Alex.

As the time for his performance neared, Alex retreated backstage, the din of the crowd muffled by the heavy curtains. Miss Electra came to join him, her presence a comforting constant in his tumultuous journey. "You've turned your trials into triumphs, darling," she said, adjusting his costume—a brilliant ensemble of lights and reflective materials designed to dazzle under the spotlight. "Tonight, you shine for all of us, for everyone who's ever been afraid to stand up and be seen."

Stepping onto the stage, Alex took a deep breath as the intro music began, a soft, haunting melody that gradually built into a crescendo. His body moved almost on its own accord, each step and gesture a beat in the story he was telling. The crowd watched, rapt, as he transformed pain into beauty, his dance a powerful narrative of falling and rising again.

Mid-performance, Alex's eyes caught a figure at the back of the crowd, a face obscured by the brim of a hat, a chill of recognition coursing through him. The threats, the fear, the danger—it all crystallized into that single, ominous figure watching him. But as the music swelled, and the crowd cheered, Alex found a new resolve. He danced harder, spoke louder, his voice ringing clear over the throng: "We are here, we are seen, and we will not be silenced."

The performance ended to thunderous applause, the cheers a tangible wave of support that washed over him, reinforcing his resolve. Backstage, the queens enveloped him in hugs and praise, their earlier anxieties dissolved in the face of his triumphant declaration.

However, the shadow at the back of the crowd didn't leave Alex's thoughts. After the festival, he reported the sighting to the police, who intensified their efforts to trace the source of the threats. The investigation turned up links to a small but dangerous fringe group known for their extreme views, a lead that both alarmed and fortified Alex's determination to stand against them.

In the weeks that followed, Alex became more than a performer; he became an advocate, speaking at events about his experiences, about fear and bravery, about the light that must be protected against the encroaching dark. Each appearance, each speech, drew more support, more allies to their cause, turning what had begun as a personal battle into a broader movement for change.

As summer deepened, so did Alex's role within the community and his commitment to the House of Lavender. The house itself became a symbol of defiance, a place where fear was converted into strength, where every song and dance was a strike against intolerance.

Chapter 14

A NIGHT OF ECHOES

As the season shifted towards the end of summer, the atmosphere within the House of Lavender was one of contemplative action. Alex's public presence had grown, not just as a performer but as a beacon for those grappling with their own shadows. His advocacy work brought him into new spaces—conferences, talk shows, and community centers—where his words sparked conversations and his story inspired courage.

With this new role came a deeper realization of the responsibilities he held.

Each speech he delivered, each interview he conducted, was imbued with his earnest desire to make a difference, to turn his once-painful experiences into a ladder for others to climb towards their own light.

The House of Lavender, always a hub of creativity and support, became increasingly involved in these efforts. The queens organized community outreach programs, hosting workshops and forums on art as a tool for social change. These activities not only strengthened the bonds within the community but also solidified the house's role as a sanctuary for the marginalized.

One late August evening, as the city basked in the golden hues of the setting sun, Alex sat in the quiet of the house's sprawling garden, reflecting on the journey that had brought him here. The garden was in full bloom, the air rich with the scent of roses and jasmine, a stark contrast to the turmoil that had once defined his life. He thought about the upcoming anniversary of his arrival at the House of Lavender—a year that had transformed him in ways he could never have imagined.

Miss Electra joined him, her presence as reassuring as ever. Together, they discussed plans for the anniversary celebration, intending to mark it with an event that would celebrate not just Alex's journey but the growth and resilience of the entire house. "It will be a night of stories and songs," Miss Electra declared, her eyes twinkling with excitement. "A celebration of every battle fought and every fear overcome."

The event, dubbed "A Night of Echoes," quickly took shape. Alex threw himself into the preparations, designing a program that included performances by each of the house members, showcasing their individual and collective talents. He was to close the show with a new piece, one that he had been secretly working on for months—a performance that encapsulated his gratitude and hope for the future.

As the day of the event arrived, the House of Lavender was transformed. Lights strung through the trees cast a warm glow over the assembled guests, a mix of community members, activists, and friends who had supported them throughout the year. The performances were poignant, each one a thread in the rich tapestry of their shared experiences.

When it was Alex's turn to take the stage, the garden fell into a reverent silence. His performance was a powerful fusion of dance and spoken word, telling the story of a man who had walked through darkness to find his light. The final lines of his monologue, delivered with a raw honesty that brought tears to many eyes, were a pledge to continue fighting, to continue shining, for as long as he had breath.

The applause that followed was more than appreciation—it was affirmation. The community's response reinforced the impact of Alex's work and the importance of the House of Lavender as a beacon of hope and resistance.

The celebration lingered into the night, filled with laughter and music, a stark reminder of how far they had all come. For Alex, it was a moment of profound fulfillment, a realization that his new life was not just about surviving but thriving.

As summer faded into fall, Alex continued his work with renewed vigor, knowing that each step he took not only carved a path for himself but also for those who would follow. The House of Lavender stood proudly in the city, its doors open, its lights bright—a home, a haven, and a testament to the enduring power of community and courage.

Chapter 15

ECHOES OF TOMORROW

As autumn painted the city in shades of orange and gold, the House of Lavender reflected a sense of accomplishment and reflective peace. Alex's journey, once marked by fear and flight, had evolved into one of advocacy and influence. Yet, the approach of winter brought with it a contemplative mood, prompting Alex to consider the future and the lasting impact he hoped to leave.

The close of the year was nearing, and with it came thoughts of sustainability—how to ensure that the work he had started would continue to flourish, even if he chose one day to step back from the spotlight. The community he had built around him was strong, but he knew the importance of fostering leadership and initiative in others.

During one crisp evening, the House of Lavender held a meeting, convened by Alex and Miss Electra, to discuss the future. The room was filled with faces that had become not just familiar but familial. Each person there had been touched by the house's efforts, whether through outreach, performance, or personal support. Alex shared his vision for a mentorship program, an initiative designed to empower upcoming artists and activists within the community. The idea was met with enthusiastic approval, and plans were swiftly put into motion.

The mentorship program, named "Echoes of Tomorrow," was designed to train and support individuals who could carry forward the mission of the House of Lavender. Workshops, seminars, and personal mentorship sessions were scheduled, and the response from the community was overwhelmingly positive. The house buzzed with renewed energy, as experienced members took on mentoring roles, sharing their knowledge and skills.

As winter deepened and the first snow fell, the city slowed, but the House of Lavender remained a vibrant hub of activity. Alex found great satisfaction in his role as a mentor, seeing in his mentees the same fears and hopes that had once consumed him. It was during one particularly reflective mentoring session that he realized how much he had changed. "The greatest echo we can create," he told a young mentee, "is the one that resonates in the lives of others after we are gone."

The year concluded with a grand event hosted by the House of Lavender, celebrating the success of the mentorship program's inaugural months. The evening was a spectacular showcase of talent and transformation, with mentees taking the stage to share their art and their stories. Alex watched from the wings, a proud smile on his face, his heart full.

As the clock struck midnight, signaling the start of a new year, Alex stood before the gathered crowd, raising a glass in a toast. "To the echoes of tomorrow," he declared, "may they be as bright and bold as the journey we've embarked on together."

The applause that followed rang out into the night, a sound that carried with it the promise of continued growth and community. As the guests celebrated, Alex stepped outside, letting the quiet of the snowy evening envelop him. He looked up at the stars, a vast canvas that reminded him of the infinite possibilities that lay ahead. He knew that whatever challenges and opportunities the future held, he was ready to meet them with the same courage and determination that had guided him this far.

ABOUT THE AUTHOR

Valentina Marquis is a vibrant new voice in contemporary literature, known for her captivating narratives that explore themes of identity, transformation, and the human experience. Born and raised in the cultural mosaic of New Orleans, her writing is infused with a passion for storytelling that transcends conventional boundaries and speaks to a diverse audience.

Valentina's journey into the world of literature was as unconventional as her stories. With a background in theater and performance art, she brings a dramatic flair and deep emotional insight to her writing. Her works often delve into the lives of those on the margins, bringing their stories to the forefront with empathy and integrity.

"House of Lavender" marks her debut into the literary world, drawing from her extensive experience with the LGBTQ+ community and her deep respect for the art of drag. Through her vivid characters and poignant narratives, Valentina seeks to challenge perceptions, open hearts, and celebrate the courage of those who live boldly.

Beyond her writing, Valentina is an avid supporter of LGBTQ+ rights and works closely with several organizations to advocate for equality and representation. She is also a frequent speaker at literary festivals and events, where she discusses the intersection of art and activism.

Valentina currently resides in San Francisco, where she lives with her two dogs, a bookshelf full of stories, and an ever-growing collection of vintage typewriters. When she's not writing or advocating, she enjoys exploring the vibrant arts scene in her city and experimenting with culinary arts at home.

"House of Lavender" is not just a book but a window into the struggles and triumphs of an extraordinary community, penned by an author who believes in the transformative power of storytelling. With each page, Valentina Marquis invites readers to look beyond the surface and see the beauty in diversity and the strength in authenticity.

ACKNOWLEDGMENTS

Writing this book has been a journey of discovery, celebration, and profound gratitude. It is a journey that could not have been undertaken alone, and this page is dedicated to all those who have walked with me along this path.

First and foremost, I extend my deepest thanks to the vibrant community of drag queens—your stories, struggles, and triumphs are the heartbeat of this narrative. You have shown the world the true meaning of bravery, beauty, and resilience. Thank you for your courage in breaking barriers and your boundless creativity, which have inspired not just this book but countless lives around the globe.

To the House of Lavender, both a figment and a reflection of reality, thank you for providing a fictional sanctuary where truth and artifice dance in beautiful harmony. This book owes its spirit to the safe spaces that real-life houses and bars provide, places where many find solace and strength.

A special thank you to the countless activists and advocates who fight tirelessly for LGBTQ+ rights. Your determination and advocacy pave the way for a brighter, more inclusive future. This book is imbued with your spirit and perseverance.

To my friends and family—your love and encouragement have been my anchor and my guiding light. Thank you for standing by me, for believing in this story, and for reminding me of the importance of telling it.

And to you, the readers, who embark on this journey with Alex and the unforgettable cast of characters—thank you for your openness and willingness to explore the depths of these pages. May you find laughter, tears, and a renewed sense of hope within this story.

Lastly, I want to acknowledge anyone who has ever felt unseen or misunderstood. May you find in this book a reminder that you are not alone, that your story matters, and that there are communities waiting to embrace you with open arms.

This book is a tapestry woven from many threads, each one vital to the integrity and richness of the whole. Thank you all for being part of this incredible tapestry.

With all my gratitude and love.

Valentina